THE
Toothpaste
MILLIONAIRE

By Jean Merrill
Illustrations by Jan Palmer

Bank Street

Prepared by the Bank Street College of Education
Houghton Mifflin Company, Boston

Library of Congress Cataloging-in-Publication data is on file.

HC ISBN-10: 0-618-75924-7
PAP ISBN-10: 0-618-75925-5

HC ISBN-13: 978-0-618-75924-8
PAP ISBN-13: 978-0-618-75925-5

Printed in the United States of America
QUM 10 9 8 7 6 5 4 3

THE
Toothpaste
MILLIONAIRE

Contents

My Friend Rufus

This is the story of my friend Rufus Mayflower and how he got to be a millionaire. With a little help from me. With a lot of help from me, as a matter of fact. But the idea was Rufus's.

Rufus's idea wasn't to become a millionaire. Just to make toothpaste. He was twelve and in the sixth grade at the time. By the time Rufus goes into the eighth grade this fall, he'll have over a million dollars in the bank.

I don't suppose you know too many eighth graders who are millionaires, and you wouldn't know Rufus was one to look at him. He still wears the same old blue sweater.

First, I'll tell you how Rufus and I got to be such good friends, since I'm white and he's black, and this seems to surprise some people.

Two years ago the company my father works for moved from Connecticut to Cleveland, Ohio. In Connecticut we lived in the suburbs.

You may not believe it, but up to the time we moved to Cleveland, I had never met a black person. There weren't any black families where we lived in Connecticut. But in East Cleveland, where we live now, there are quite a few. East Cleveland is an old neighborhood with big houses and lawns and trees that look a hundred years old. My father says you can't buy a new house built as well as these big old houses.

Our house in Cleveland has a lot more rooms than our house in Connecticut. There's a room called a conservatory, which is just for plants! And there's a huge laundry room and workshop, which came in handy when Rufus decided to make toothpaste.

I didn't meet Rufus until several weeks after school started. Sometimes it's hard making friends in a new neighborhood, and the kids on my block weren't too friendly at first. It was okay at school, but after school and on weekends, it was lonely.

There wasn't anybody to hang around with but my brother James, and he isn't interested in anything but model cars. If you've ever had a brother who's crazy about model cars, you know his conversation isn't very interesting. You can't even understand it. It's all about camshafts and gear ratios and rpms.

I know that if you want to make friends, you have to be friendly. And I tried.

There were two girls about my age, Clem and Josie, who lived in the house next door, and I thought it would be easy to make friends with them. One afternoon I saw them watching me pick apples from this nice old apple tree we have in the backyard, and I invited them to come over and pick some apples if they wanted. But they said no.

Another time when Clem broke her badminton racket, I called over to ask if she wanted to borrow one of mine. But she didn't.

Maybe they didn't like apples or were tired of playing badminton. But I had the feeling it was that they didn't want to get involved with me. Maybe because I was white.

One of the nice things about Rufus is this: He doesn't seem to mind that I'm white and he's black. He doesn't even mind that I'm a girl. My brother James, though, can hardly stand it that I'm a girl. This can be pretty annoying in a nine-year-old boy.

With Rufus I didn't even have to try to make friends. It was as if we always had been, from the first day I met him. I was riding my bike to school, and the strap that I use to hold my books on the back of the bike broke. I heard my books go thunking all over the street.

Well, I pulled up to the curb and was trying to figure out how to rescue the books. Papers from my notebook were blowing all over the place.

Every time I ducked into the street to grab a paper, cars started honking their horns. It was the rush hour, and nobody wanted to stop.

Suddenly this kid on a bike pulls up behind me. He jumps off his bike and runs into the middle of the street and puts up his hands like a traffic cop.

"Take your time," he says to me. Then, when he gets the traffic under control, he helps me pick up all my stuff.

Some kids who lived on my street were standing on the sidewalk laughing at the two of us crawling under cars. One of them yelled, "Hey, Rufus, you'll be late for school."

Rufus didn't pay any attention, except to explain to me, "That's my name—Rufus."

Rufus tried to fix my broken book strap. But when he tied it together, it wasn't long enough to go around the books.

"Never mind," he said. "I'll put them in my saddlebags."

Rufus had these beautiful blue nylon saddlebags that fit over the carrier of his bike.

"Those are neat," I said. "Where'd you get them?"

"Made 'em," Rufus said.

He stuffed my books into the top of the saddlebags. "Can't spill out of there," he said. "C'mon. We'll see who's late for school." He waved at the kids on the sidewalk as we zoomed past them on our bikes.

When I pulled up beside him at a red light, Rufus said, "I'll make you some if you get the material."

"Some what?" I said.

"Saddlebags," Rufus said. "You can get water-proof nylon in red, orange, blue, or black at Vince's Army & Navy."

At the next traffic light, he said, "You don't need to buy leather for the straps. I've got some left over from making my saddlebags. All you need is the nylon."

Rufus was in my math class. I hadn't noticed him before the day he picked up my books. So I was surprised when he walked into the math class later the same day.

Halfway through the class, someone behind me passed me a note. It said:

You will need 2 1/4 yards of 36-inch-wide nylon, which is 97¢ a yard at Vince's, which will come to $2.18 1/4, plus sales tax.

At the end of the note was a neat little drawing. It showed the pattern for the saddlebags laid out on the 36-inch-wide material with the length and width of each piece carefully marked.

I was turning around to let Rufus know that I got the note when Mr. Conti, our math teacher, called out my name.

"Kate MacKinstrey," he said, "would you please bring that note to me."

Mr. Conti's way of cutting down on notes in his class is to read aloud every one he spots going around. It was just my luck to get caught with the first note anybody had ever passed me in his class.

The kids around me were snickering. There hadn't been a juicy note to laugh at for a week. And I guess because I was a new kid, everybody was watching to see how I'd manage in a tight spot.

The last thing I wanted to do was to get Rufus into trouble. I tried to look very innocent and said, "It's not exactly a note, Mr. Conti."

"Well, what *exactly* is it?" Mr. Conti asked.

I felt my face getting red. But I stuck to my explanation. "It's a kind of math problem," I said.

"Then I'd be even *more* interested in seeing it," Mr. Conti said.

There wasn't anything I could do except take the note up to Mr. Conti. He read it to himself and then looked up kind of surprised.

"Believe it or not," he said to the class, "it *is* a math problem. The answer looks right. But I think we'd better check it out."

And what happened then was that Mr. Conti went to the chalkboard and copied off Rufus's pattern for the saddlebags. He wrote in the measurements for each piece of the pattern—16" x 14 1/2" and 16" x 8 1/4" and so on. Rufus had everything down to fractions of an inch.

Then Mr. Conti asked the class: "How many yards of thirty-six-inch-wide material would you need to cut out all the pieces for this pattern? And how much will the material cost at ninety-seven cents a yard?"

The class groaned.

Somebody wanted to know what the pattern was for. That stumped Mr. Conti.

"A blouse, I suppose," he said.

He checked with me. "A blouse?"

"Yes," I said. "A blue blouse."

I hoped Rufus wouldn't think I was making fun of him. I sneaked a look at the back of the room, but I couldn't tell what Rufus was thinking. He was scrunched over his notebook as if he were working very hard on the problem.

The answer looked very simple the way Rufus had the pattern all drawn out in the note. But it took the rest of the class the whole *period* to work out their answers.

And everybody's answer was different! The class had that nylon costing anywhere from $2.91 up to over $10—partly because no one could figure out how to fit the pieces of the pattern on the material without wasting a lot of cloth.

I never did have to tell Mr. Conti who wrote the note. I think he might have had an idea, though, because Rufus's answers were the only ones that matched those in the note.

When I went to pick up my bike after school, there was another note taped onto the handlebars. In this note were two maps. One map showed how to get to Vince's Army & Navy on Merchant's Row, and the other showed how to get to Rufus's house from Vince's. Rufus lived only about three blocks from me.

I rode straight down to Vince's after school. The store was in a part of town where I'd never been before. But Rufus's map was easy to follow.

I got $2^1/4$ yards of the same blue nylon that Rufus's bags were made of. Then I followed the other map to his house.

I didn't know if Rufus expected me to show up with the nylon so soon. But when I knocked at the door, Rufus's mother said, "You must be Kate. Rufus is in the kitchen."

In the kitchen Rufus had the pattern for the saddlebags all laid out. He had already cut out the leather straps to fasten the bags with and had put buckles on the straps.

Rufus gave me some pins and told me to pin the pattern shapes to the nylon. Then he cut out the pattern and set up his mother's sewing machine and sewed all the pieces together.

But I still wouldn't have believed it if you had told me that within a year and a half, Rufus would be a millionaire. My father says it should have been obvious that anyone who could figure out, within a fourth of a yard, how much material you need for a saddlebag could make a million dollars making toothpaste.

By suppertime, the saddlebags were finished. I was amazed.

But I'd never known anyone before who could make saddlebags. Let alone toothpaste.

Toothpaste and Eye Shadow

I remember the morning Rufus got the idea for toothpaste. He had to do some shopping for his mother, and I went along with him. We were in the Cut-Rate Drugstore, because toothpaste was one of the things on Rufus's list.

I was looking at some name-brand eye shadow that was on sale, when I heard Rufus say, "Seventy-nine cents! Seventy-nine cents for a six-inch tube of toothpaste. That's crazy!"

"It's better than eighty-nine cents," I said. I pointed to some 89¢ tubes farther down the shelf.

"That's even crazier," Rufus said. "What can be in those tubes anyway? Just some peppermint flavoring and some paste."

"Maybe the paste is expensive to make," I said.

"Paste!" Rufus said. "You don't need powdered gold to make paste. Paste is made out of everyday ordinary stuff. Didn't you ever make paste?"

"Toothpaste?" I said.

"I mean just plain paste for pasting things together," Rufus said. "My Grandma Mayflower showed me how to make paste when I was four years old."

"How do you do it?" I asked.

"Simple," Rufus said. "You just take a little flour and starch and cook them with a little water till the mixture has a nice pasty feel. Then you can use it to paste pictures in a scrapbook. Or paste up wallpaper."

"But you couldn't brush your teeth with *that*," I said.

"Well, I don't know," Rufus said. "I never tried. But I bet toothpaste isn't any harder to make. Anyway, I'm not paying any seventy-nine cents for a tube of toothpaste."

Rufus crossed toothpaste off his mother's shopping list.

"But your mother said to get toothpaste . . ." I said. "You can't help it if it's expensive."

"I'll make her some," Rufus said. "I bet I can make a gallon of it for seventy-nine cents."

"Maybe even for seventy-eight and one-eighth cents," I said.

Rufus laughed. "Maybe," he said.

"Hey," I said. "Do you think you could make eye shadow, too?"

It suddenly struck me that sixty-nine cents for a smidge of eye shadow about as big as a nickel—and that was the cut-rate sale price—was a little bit expensive, too.

"Eye shadow's a kind of pasty stuff," I told Rufus. "Maybe if you just added coloring to toothpaste . . ."

"Maybe," Rufus said. "But what's the point? Nobody really needs eye shadow. If anybody's crazy enough to pay sixty-nine cents for something he doesn't *need*, I can't be bothered about him. But everybody needs to brush his teeth. If I could make a good, cheap toothpaste, that would be worth doing."

I decided not to buy any eye shadow. Rufus was right. Who needed it?

In addition to which, I didn't even *like* eye shadow. I had tried it, and I didn't like the feel of it or the bother of putting it on. But some of my friends were buying eye shadow and trying out new shades and talking about which brand was the best, and I just got into the habit of going along with them.

"Rufus," I said, as we rode our bikes home, "I'm going to tell you something I've never told anyone before. I hate eye shadow. I really *hate* it."

"I don't care too much about it one way or the other myself," Rufus said.

"And it just occurred to me," I said, "that if I never buy any eye shadow for the rest of my life, I'll probably save at least ten dollars a year. If I live till I'm eighty, that's seven hundred dollars."

"Great!" Rufus said.

"And if I could save money on toothpaste, too . . ." I said. "Wow!" I was thinking about how easy it would be to get rich just by not buying things the stores want you to buy.

"How much do you think it would cost us to make our own toothpaste?" I asked Rufus.

"I don't know," Rufus said. "But I just thought of something else. You know what I used to brush my teeth with when I stayed at my Grandma

Mayflower's in North Carolina? You know what my grandma uses to brush her teeth?"

"What?" I asked.

"Bicarbonate of soda," Rufus said. "Just plain old baking soda. You just put a little of the soda powder on your toothbrush."

"*Bicarb?*" I said. "That's the stuff my mother tries to give me when I feel sick to my stomach. Bicarbonate of soda in water. I can't *stand* the taste."

"Really?" Rufus said. "To me bicarb has a nice refreshing taste. Sort of like 7-Up without the lemon-lime flavor."

"But who wants to drink 7-Up without the lemon-lime flavor?" I said. "That's the whole *point* of 7-Up."

"I guess you're right," Rufus said. "I guess that's why more people don't brush their teeth with bicarb."

Peppermint, Clove, Vanilla, Curry, or Almond?

The next afternoon when I stopped by Rufus's house to borrow his bike pump, he had about fifty bowls and pans scattered around the kitchen.

"What are you making?" I asked.

"I already made it," Rufus said.

He handed me a spoon and a bowl with some white stuff in it. I took a spoonful.

"Don't eat it," Rufus said. "Just taste it. Rub a little on your teeth."

I tried a little.

"How does it taste?" Rufus asked.

"Not bad," I said. "Better than the kind my mother buys in the pink and white striped tube. How'd you get it to taste so good?"

"A drop of peppermint oil," Rufus said. "But I've got other flavors, too."

He pushed three other pots of paste across the table. The first one had a spicy taste.

"Clove-flavored," Rufus said. "You like it?"

"I don't know," I said. "It's interesting."

"Try this one."

The next sample had a sweet taste. "Vanilla," I guessed.

"Right," Rufus said.

"I like vanilla," I said. "In milk shakes. Or ice cream. But it doesn't seem quite right in toothpaste. Too sweet."

"This one won't be too sweet," Rufus said, handing me another sample.

"*Eeegh,*" I said and ran to the sink to wash out my mouth. "What did you put in *that?*"

"Curry powder," Rufus said. "You don't like it? I thought it tasted like a good shrimp curry."

"Maybe it does," I said, "but I don't like curry."

Rufus looked disappointed. "I don't suppose you'd like it almond-flavored, either," he said. "I made some of that, too, but I decided not too many people would take to almond."

"What flavor is in that big plastic pan?" I asked. "You've got enough of that kind to frost twenty-seven cakes."

"That's no kind yet," Rufus said. "That's just seventy-nine cents' worth of the stuff that goes in the paste. I didn't want to flavor it till I figured out the best taste."

"What does it taste like plain?" I asked.

"Well," Rufus said, "mostly you taste the bicarb."

"Bicarb!" I said. "You mean all this stuff I've been tasting has got bicarbonate of soda in it?"

Rufus grinned. "Yeah," he said. "It's probably good for your stomach as well as your teeth."

Know what I did when I got home that night? I mixed up some bicarbonate of soda in water. It wasn't that I was feeling sick. It was just that Rufus gave me this inspiration.

What I did was to add a few drops of vanilla and a little sugar to the bicarb water. And you know what? It tasted something like cream soda. You'd never know you were drinking bicarb.

And I like cream soda even better than 7-Up.

CHAPTER

5

Another Nice Thing About Rufus

I forgot to mention another nice thing about Rufus. The afternoon Rufus let me sample his first batch of toothpaste, he was trying to figure out how many tubes of toothpaste it would make.

We looked at a medium-sized tube of toothpaste.

"You must have enough for ten tubes in that plastic bowl," I guessed.

"More, I bet," Rufus said.

"Why don't you squeeze the toothpaste in the tube into a measuring cup and then measure the stuff in the bowl," I suggested.

"That would be a waste of toothpaste," Rufus said. "We couldn't get it back in the tube." Rufus hates to waste anything.

"I have a better idea," he said. "I'll pack into a square pan the toothpaste I made. Then I can figure out how many cubic inches of toothpaste we have. And you can figure out how many cubic inches of toothpaste are in the tube."

"But the tube is round, Rufus," I said. "I can't measure cubic inches unless something is cube-shaped."

Rufus thought a minute. "Maybe we can squeeze the tube into a cube shape," he said.

I thought that was brilliant. But then I had another idea.

"Rufus," I said. "It says on the tube that it contains three and a quarter ounces of toothpaste. Why couldn't we just weigh your paste and divide by three and a quarter to see how many tubes it would make?"

"Hey—we could!" Rufus said. "You are *smart*, Kate. I'm always doing things the hard way."

That's what is really so nice about Rufus. It's not just that he gets great ideas like making toothpaste. But if *you* have a good idea, he says so.

I was pleased that I had thought of a simpler way of measuring the toothpaste, but I told Rufus, "I wish I was smart enough even to *think* of a hard way of doing something."

I *never* would have thought of measuring toothpaste in cubic inches. Partly because I never can remember exactly how to figure cubic inches. And I certainly wouldn't have thought of making a round tube cube-shaped. Would you?

Anyway it turned out Rufus had made about forty tubes of toothpaste for 79¢.

CHAPTER 6

Another Math Problem

Before I finished breakfast the next morning, there was a knock on the door. It was Rufus. He was very excited.

"Kate!" he said. "Do you know what the population of the United States is?"

"No," I said. I never know things like that.

My father looked up from his paper. "According to the most recent census—over two hundred million," he said to Rufus. My father always knows things like that.

"You're right," Rufus said. "And by now, it must be even bigger."

"Probably," my father said. "The growing population is a very serious matter. Have you thought much about that problem, Rufus?"

"Not yet, Mr. MacKinstrey," Rufus said. "At the moment, I was thinking mainly about toothpaste. I was thinking that everybody in the United States probably uses about one tube of toothpaste a month."

"Probably," my father said.

"And if they do," Rufus said, "how many tubes of toothpaste are sold in a year?"

My father thought for a second. "Roughly two and a half billion tubes."

"Right!" Rufus said.

I hate people who can multiply in their heads. Except that my father and Rufus are two of the people I like best in the world. How do you explain that?

I really don't like math at all, even when I have a paper and pencil and all the time in the world to figure something out.

And at the same time I look forward every day to Mr. Conti's math class. And how do you explain that, since that's the class where I'm always getting in trouble?

For example, the same day my father brought up the population explosion, there's Mr. Conti in math class saying:

"Kate MacKinstrey, would you please bring me that note."

"Well, it isn't exactly a note, Mr. Conti."

"I see," says Mr. Conti. "I suppose it's another math problem."

"It looks like a math problem, Mr. Conti."

The message from Rufus that Mr. Conti got to read that day said:

If there are 2 1/2 billion tubes of toothpaste sold in the U.S. in one year, and 1 out of 10 people switched to a new brand, how many tubes of the new brand would they be buying?

The right answer is 250 million. It took the class a while to figure that out. Some people have trouble remembering how many zeros there are in a billion.

Then there was a second part to the note:

If the inventor of the new toothpaste made a profit of 1¢ a tube on his toothpaste, what would his profit be at the end of a year?

And it turns out that the inventor of this new toothpaste would make $2.5 million in profit!

The Joe Smiley Show

Well, that's how Rufus's toothpaste business started. With Rufus figuring out that if he sold the toothpaste for only a penny more than it cost him to make—it cost him about 2¢ a tube—that he'd soon have millions of customers.

He had to start in a small way, of course. When he started his business, Rufus packed the toothpaste in baby food jars. A baby food jar holds about as much as a big tube, and the jars didn't cost him anything.

People with babies were glad to save jars for Rufus, as nobody had thought of a way of instantly recycling baby food jars before. When Rufus put a sign on the bulletin board at school saying he could use the jars, kids brought us hundreds of them.

We sterilized and filled the jars. When we had about five hundred jars, Rufus and I stuffed our saddlebags with as many as they would hold and rode our bikes around the neighborhood selling the toothpaste.

We sold quite a few jars. At only 3¢ a jar, most people felt they could afford to give it a try, and most of the customers said it was good toothpaste.

Still, I could not see how Rufus was going to get rich on 3¢ toothpaste unless millions of people knew about it. Then I had this idea about how he could get some free advertising.

Everybody in Cleveland watches a program called *The Joe Smiley Show*. On the show, Joe interviews people who have interesting hobbies.

I wrote Joe Smiley a letter telling him I had this friend who had a hobby of making toothpaste and could make about a two-year supply for the price of one tube. And Joe Smiley called up Rufus to ask if he would be on the show.

Rufus was very good on the show, though I was afraid that he never would get around to talking about the toothpaste. I was worried because when Joe Smiley asked Rufus how he had learned to make toothpaste, Rufus started telling about his Grandmother Mayflower.

He told not only about the scrapbook paste, but

about how his Grandma Mayflower had made her own furnace out of two 100-gallon oil barrels. Joe Smiley was so interested in that furnace that it was hard to get him off the subject of Rufus's grandmother.

Rufus told about his grandmother taming raccoons, woodchucks, mice, chipmunks, and catbirds. And, of course, about her brushing her teeth with plain baking soda. But the story I liked best was about his grandmother's name.

It seems Mayflower was his grandmother's *whole* name. She didn't have any last name till she got married. Then she took her husband's name, which was Proctor, and was known as Mrs. Mayflower Proctor.

But Rufus's grandmother never did like the name Proctor, because it was a slave name. (Rufus explained that back when there were slaves, a black man was sometimes called by the name of the white family who owned him.)

So when Mayflower's husband died, she dropped the Proctor part of her name, and she and her children went back to being Mayflowers. Then

Social Security came along and said she had to have a first name and a last name on her Social Security card. But rather than let the government put her down with a slave name, Mrs. Mayflower wrote the Social Security people and signed herself Mrs. May Flower, with a space between the "May" and the "Flower."

I love that story. In fact, I'm seriously thinking about changing my name to Mac Kinstrey, as I don't care too much for Kathryn. Mac sounds like a boy's name, and boys' names usually sound a lot more forceful than girls' names to me.

But I'm getting off the subject of toothpaste, just as Rufus did on *The Joe Smiley Show*. You wouldn't think all that stuff about Rufus's grandmother would sell toothpaste. But then, as my father pointed out, you wouldn't think Rufus's way of advertising the toothpaste would sell toothpaste, either.

Joe Smiley is the kind of guy who is always saying things are the "greatest" thing he ever heard of. Or the most "fantastic." If a girl comes on his show in a pink coat that Joe thinks is attractive, he'll say,

"That's the most fantastic coat!" There's nothing that special about the coat. He just means it's nice.

What I mean is, he exaggerates. And everybody Joe has on his show is one of the greatest people he ever met or has done the most fantastic thing.

So when Joe does get to Rufus's toothpaste, he naturally gives it this big build-up. Which is what I was counting on. And what does Rufus do?

The conversation went something like this:

JOE: Now, Rufus, this fantastic toothpaste you make—I suppose it has a special, secret formula.

RUFUS: No. It's made out of stuff anybody can buy for a few cents and mix up at home in a few minutes.

JOE: Fantastic! And, of course, it's much better than the kind you buy at the store.

RUFUS: I don't know about that. But it tastes pretty good. And for about two cents you can make as much as you get in a seventy-nine-cent tube.

Chapter 7

JOE: Fantastic! And where can people get some of this great toothpaste?

RUFUS: If they live in East Cleveland, I'll deliver it to them on my bike. Three ounces costs three cents—it costs me two cents to make and I make a one cent profit. If anyone outside East Cleveland wants some, I'll have to charge three cents plus postage.

JOE: Fantastic! And what do you call this marvelous new product?

RUFUS: Toothpaste.

JOE: Just toothpaste? It doesn't have a name like Sparkle or Shine or Sensation or White Lightning or Personality Plus?

RUFUS: No, it's just plain Toothpaste. It doesn't do anything sensational such as improve your smile or your personality. It just keeps your teeth clean.

Who would have thought that telling people toothpaste wouldn't do one thing for their personalities would sell toothpaste?

But three days after Rufus was on *The Joe Smiley*

Show, he got 689 orders for Toothpaste. One came all the way from Venice, California, from a man who happened to be telephoning his daughter while she was watching the show in Cleveland. The daughter said, "There's a kid here who's selling toothpaste for three cents a jar." And her father ordered three dozen jars.

Fantastic!

There's a song that goes, "I'll get by with a little help from my friends." Rufus couldn't have filled all the orders that poured in after *The Joe Smiley Show* without some help from his friends.

Luckily, after the show a lot of kids began coming around every night after school to see how Rufus was doing. Rufus said they could hang around, but they'd have to help us pack toothpaste.

We were working in our laundry room now. When Rufus's mother decided she couldn't have her kitchen turned into a full-time toothpaste factory, I asked my mother if we could use the workshop at the end of our laundry room.

My brother James had been using the workshop for his model cars, and my mother was glad for an excuse to make James move his workshop into the attic. James is not very neat.

My father helped us build two long tables for the laundry room, and once Rufus and I got all the jars and supplies set up, the place really did look like a factory.

Some afternoons we had six or eight kids on the production line. Some of the kids were from school, and some lived on my block, like Josie and Clem, the two girls from next door.

Josie and Clem were at my house almost every night now. I guess they decided that if I was a friend of Rufus, I was okay. I was glad they were coming over so often, as Rufus and I were getting a little tired of washing so many jars. I never was crazy about washing dishes.

"Hey, Rufus," Josie said one night when she and I had washed about 200 jars. "What would you do if you had to pay us to wash all these jars for you?"

"How about that, Rufus?" Clem said. "You couldn't sell that toothpaste for three cents if you had to pay us what we're worth."

Rufus thought about that.

"Well, I sure don't have enough profits to pay anybody yet," he said. "And I've got to use my first profits to buy more stuff to make more toothpaste. But I'll tell you what I will do. I'll give you all some stock in my company. At the end of the year, every stockholder will get a share of the year's profits."

Clem thought Rufus was kidding. But he was serious.

Rufus had this game called Stock Market. It's something like Monopoly. With every Stock Market game, you get these stock certificates that you can trade with other players. In Rufus's game there were 1,000 shares of stock worth $100 a share. The certificates came in 1, 10, 50, and 100 shares. Rufus brought the stock certificates over to my house the next day to show us.

"Here's how it will work," he said. "Anybody that puts in a hundred hours helping me make toothpaste gets a share of stock worth one hundred dollars, which will entitle him to a share of the company's profits. How much profit depends on how many shares of stock he owns."

Rufus had made up a chart with the names of all of his friends who had helped so far. He put down the number of hours they had already worked.

"Kate's already worked over two hundred hours," Rufus said, "so she gets to be the first stockholder."

Rufus wrote my name on two $100 stock certificates. "With those two shares of stock, Kate should get five thousand dollars if the company's profits work out the way I plan."

"Five thousand dollars!" I said. "Are you sure that's right, Rufus?"

Rufus laughed. "We'll let Mr. Conti check it out tomorrow." And we did:

"Kate MacKinstrey, would you, please, bring that note to me?"

"Well, it's not exactly a note, Mr. Conti."

Etcetera.

You get the picture.

Mr. Conti's class figured out that if Rufus was right about the $2.5 million profit he figured he could make, every owner of one share of stock would make $2,500. An owner of ten shares would make $25,000. And so on.

It sounded so good that everybody in our math class wanted to sign up to work for shares. Even

Mr. Conti told Rufus he'd give us a hand if we needed extra help on Saturdays.

"When the money starts rolling in," Rufus said, "we may need some help in adding it up."

Mr. Conti also gave Rufus some advice. He told Rufus that he shouldn't give out more than 499 shares of the stock.

"You have to keep five hundred and one shares yourself to keep control of how you want your company run," Mr. Conti said. "Otherwise the other stockholders could outvote you."

"What did Mr. Conti mean—outvote you?" I asked Rufus later.

"Maybe vote to sell toothpaste for seventy-nine cents," Rufus said. "Which would be against my principles."

Naturally, I promised Rufus I would never vote to do that.

It was my brother James, of all people, who helped me solve the problem of what to get Rufus for his birthday. He saw the ad about aluminum tubes in the *Cleveland Plain Dealer* and called it to my attention. It's one of the few helpful things James has ever done for me.

I was looking for a birthday present for Rufus. I decided what Rufus really needed at this point in his business career was some toothpaste tubes.

Rufus and I had been having some arguments about the baby food jars. A lot of customers seemed surprised at the idea of a toothpaste in a jar. It seemed a little strange.

"It's like peanut butter coming in a tube," I told Rufus.

Rufus's reaction was "Why *don't* they put peanut butter in tubes? You wouldn't need a knife to spread it."

Josie and Clem agreed with me about the jars. Clem pointed out to Rufus that jars were heavier than tubes. "If you're going to be mailing three dozen jars all the way to Venice, California, you ought to think about the postage costs," she said.

"And another thing," Josie said. "If everybody in a family is dipping his toothbrush in the same jar, it isn't too sanitary."

"Everybody can have his own jar," Rufus said. "It would be good for business if we could sell five or six jars to every family."

"The jars would get mixed up," I said.

"People could write their names on them," Rufus said.

"They could," I said. "But with a big family, there isn't room for all those jars on the bathroom shelf. And even if there were, my brother James would always reach for the first jar."

"Your brother James is a special problem," Rufus said.

At least we agreed on that.

I don't think we convinced Rufus about the jars. But I decided I would take a chance on getting him some toothpaste tubes, just to see if they would improve sales.

Did you ever try to buy a few toothpaste tubes? You can't.

I tried hardware stores. Drugstores. Department stores. I couldn't find any place that sold empty tubes. And by the time anybody is finished with an old toothpaste tube, you can't really use it again, as you can a baby food jar.

A man in a hardware store finally explained to me that an empty tube is not a retail item. He said I would have to go to a tube manufacturer.

I found some tube manufacturers listed in the Yellow Pages. And I wrote to one of them, the Tuxedo Tube & Container Corp. in Paramus, New Jersey, to ask how much a small box of medium-sized tubes would cost.

The district sales manager of Tuxedo wrote me a nice letter back explaining that their minimum orders were for 10,000 tubes. If I wanted that many, the price would be about 5¢ a tube. Also, they would be glad to quote me special prices on orders of 50,000 or 100,000.

Ten thousand toothpaste tubes seemed like a lot to start with, even though I'd got into the habit of thinking in thousands and millions since I started working with Rufus. I multiplied 10,000 by 5¢ and found Rufus's present was going to cost me $500. I decided he'd have to wait until his next birthday, after I collected all those profits on my stock certificates.

My father asked me why didn't I just get Rufus some sheets of thin lead or aluminum and let him make his own tubes, since he was so handy at making things. But it turned out aluminum sheets weren't retail items, either.

Rufus's birthday was only about a week away when James saw the auction ad. James's favorite reading is newspaper ads for bankruptcy sales.

Once James read about an auction of the "Entire Contents of a Model-Car Factory." Unfortunately, the ad was in a paper a month old, and the auction was over by the time James read about it.

Or maybe fortunately, my father says, as James probably would have gone and bought the Entire Contents. And our house could be mistaken for a model-car factory as it is. Anyway, ever since that ad, James checks the paper every morning, hoping for another model-car factory to go bankrupt.

The only auctions I'd ever been to were the kind my mother goes to, where you can buy old chairs and china cups and antique clocks. But the *Cleveland Plain Dealer* advertises auctions of the most surprising things. Printing presses. Or fifteen trailer trucks. Or Ferris wheel swings. Or 10,000 boxes of cornflakes. James reads off lists like this every morning at breakfast.

I don't generally listen to James's auction ads. Thinking about 10,000 boxes of cornflakes at breakfast can take the edge off your appetite.

"'Complete Furnishings of Funeral Parlor,'" James started off one morning.

"Half a dozen slightly shopworn coffins," my father said. "That's just what I need."

"'Miscellaneous Pharmaceutical Supplies,'" James went on, and I wasn't paying any attention until I suddenly heard the word "tubes."

"*Tubes*, did you say?" I said, almost choking on my toast.

"Yeah—tubes," James said. "Fifty gross high-quality aluminum tubes. Suitable for cosmetics, shaving creams, foods, adhesives, household cements, lubricants, leather softeners, polishes, shampoos, oil paints, insecticides, dentifrices—"

"*Dentifrices!*" I said. "That's *toothpaste!*"

"I know," James said. "I keep telling you they have good things at these auctions."

For once, James was right.

CHAPTER

10

A Gross Mistake

The auction was where I made what my father calls "a gross mistake." It was held at the Pulaski Brothers' Warehouse in downtown Cleveland.

In the room where the auction was held, there were hundreds of cartons stacked around the walls. And a lot of things you don't usually see for sale, like dentists' chairs and fire hydrants. I guess that's because they aren't retail items.

I didn't see any coffins or Ferris wheels. The day I was at Pulaski Brothers, they were selling "Odd Lots of Hardware and Miscellaneous Pharmaceutical Supplies."

The people at the auction were mostly middle-aged men. Very few women and no kids except me. A lot of the men seemed to know each other. From listening to their conversations, it sounded as though they came to Pulaski Brothers' auctions every Saturday.

I felt a little out of place until I saw somebody I knew. It was Vince, from Vince's Army & Navy, where I got the nylon for my saddlebags.

Vince didn't remember me at first, but he was very nice and said why didn't I sit down beside him. While we were waiting for the auction to begin, he bought me a cream soda.

I asked Vince what he planned to buy at the auction. "Grommets," Vince said.

"Oh," I said.

"They're a hardware item," Vince said. "You use them on tents or boats."

Vince said most of the men at the auction had small stores like his where they sold odd lots of things. I'd never heard of odd lots before. They're a little like odds and ends—but there are a lot *of* them.

They seem to be things that are left over when a business goes out of business. And they're apt to be pretty odd. Like grommets.

Vince explained to me how the auction worked. Every item to be auctioned had a number. The auctioneer sold about fifty items an hour.

Vince asked one of the Pulaski brothers what number the aluminum tubes were. They were Number 76. So I had quite a wait.

I knew from going to auctions with my mother that there was one thing you had to watch out for. You can spend all your money on something you don't need before the thing you really need comes up for sale.

When the auction started, I was on guard. I had a chance to buy a whole box of dog collars for a dollar and a quarter. But I just sat tight.

Vince bought several things. The grommets. And a box of pitons (a piton is something rock climbers use).

He also bought a barrelful of links for bike chains. He got the whole barrel for what six links would have cost at a hardware store. It was such a bargain that he gave me a handful for free.

Finally the auctioneer got to the tubes.

"Item Number Seventy-six—aluminum tubes," he announced. "High-quality tubes. Manufactured by Perfect Packaging Products. Never been used. Suitable for cosmetics, shaving creams, shampoos, foods, household cements, lubricants, oil paints, leather softeners, polishes, insecticides, dentifrices . . .”

I wished the auctioneer would stop reading off all the things you could use tubes for. I hadn't spotted anyone at the auction who looked like he might be looking for toothpaste tubes. But with all those other things you could use tubes for, I was afraid the auctioneer would have everybody wanting to buy them.

“So let's go,” said the auctioneer. “Aluminum tubes—fifty gross. How much am I bid by the gross? Bidder takes the lot.”

I tried to remember how much a gross was. Something to do with a dozen. Fifty dozen would be 600 tubes. I hadn't planned to buy that many tubes for Rufus.

“Couldn't I just bid for a couple of gross?” I whispered to Vince.

“No, you've got to buy the whole lot,” Vince said.

“Who'll bid five cents a gross?” the auctioneer was asking.

A man in the front row raised his hand. "And who'll give me six cents?" the auctioneer said.

I did some quick figuring. Six cents a dozen would be two tubes for a penny, which would be a bargain. If the price didn't go too high, maybe I could afford to buy 600 tubes. Quickly, I put up my hand.

"Six cents from the little lady in the third row," the auctioneer said.

I looked around for the little lady.

Vince nudged me. "He means you. Six cents is your bid."

"And now seven cents," the auctioneer was saying. "Who'll say seven cents?"

The man in the front row was still bidding.

"Got seven cents," the auctioneer said happily. "Who'll give eight cents?"

"I will," I called out. I only had to signal quietly with my hand, but I was afraid the auctioneer might not see me.

"Eight from the little lady," he announced. "Now I want nine cents. Who'll give nine?" The man who was bidding looked around to see who was running up the price. He gave me a sharp look. Then he motioned to the auctioneer that he would go nine.

"TEN!" I yelled, without even waiting for the auctioneer to ask.

I guess that scared the other bidder. Vince said I sounded so determined, the guy figured I was ready to run the price up to 79¢ if necessary. Anyway, he shrugged to the auctioneer that he was finished bidding.

"All through?" the auctioneer asked everybody, although there had been only the two of us bidding on the tubes. "Everybody all through? Well then—fifty gross aluminum tubes sold to the little lady for ten cents a gross."

"That's going to run you five dollars," Vince said. "You got enough money with you?"

I did. Though I hadn't planned to spend that much on Rufus's present. I would have to economize on James's birthday next month. Maybe I'd give him a couple of jars of Toothpaste.

"Anyway you got a good buy," Vince said.

I thought so, too. Six hundred tubes wasn't *really* so many, considering that Rufus got more than 600 orders from that one appearance on *The Joe Smiley Show*.

It wasn't until I took my bike around to the back of the warehouse to pick up the tubes that I discovered my mistake.

One of the Pulaski brothers wheeled out five big cartons on a hand truck. "Here you go," he said.

"Are those all mine?" I asked. I hadn't expected the boxes to be so big.

"Fifty gross is a lot of tubes," Mr. Pulaski said. "What will you do with seventy-two hundred tubes anyway?"

"*Seventy-two hundred!*" I said.

"You mean you didn't know how many tubes to a gross?" Mr. Pulaski said.

"Well, sort of . . ." I said.

But as my father keeps telling me, "sort of" knowing isn't exactly the same as "exactly" knowing.

CHAPTER

11

7,200 Toothpaste Tubes

I dialed Rufus's number. "Rufus," I said. "I have a problem."

"Math?" Rufus said. I often call him when I'm having trouble with a math assignment.

"Well, sort of," I said. "Rufus—you know how much a gross is?"

"One hundred and forty-four," Rufus said. "A dozen dozen."

"That's right," I said. "I knew it had *something* to do with a dozen, Rufus. But I thought it was just one dozen."

"What was?" Rufus asked.

"Toothpaste tubes," I said. "Rufus, I just bought fifty gross. By mistake. And the problem is that I don't think I can carry that many home on my bike."

"Oh," Rufus said.

There was a silence at the other end of the phone. It wasn't that Rufus was mad at me. He was just multiplying in his head.

"Seven thousand two hundred tubes?" Rufus asked after a minute. "Is that what you've got?"

"There are quite a few of them, Rufus," I said. "Five big boxes. I think I may need a truck."

There was another silence.

Then Rufus said, "Probably one tube weighs about an ounce. Seventy-two hundred ounces is four hundred and fifty pounds. Say about a quarter of a ton. Okay, Kate. I know what to do. Where are you?"

I told Rufus where Pulaski Brothers was. He told me to sit tight till he got there. In about an hour he showed up on his bike with four friends who delivered groceries for the A&P. The manager of the A&P had let them borrow four bike carts from the store, those bikes with a metal chest in front for carrying groceries.

The four store bikes could carry about 100 pounds each. Rufus and I put the other 50 pounds in the saddlebags on our bikes.

Chapter 11

We got all the tubes to my house and carried them to the laundry room. Rufus opened a box and took out a couple of tubes.

"You weren't supposed to see them till your birthday," I said.

"They're real nice," Rufus said. "Thank you."

Suddenly I had a terrible thought.

"Rufus," I said. "How are we going to get the toothpaste into the tubes? The hole in the top is so *small!*"

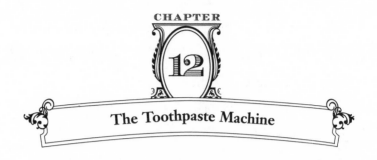

"The toothpaste goes in from the bottom, naturally," Rufus said. "Look. The bottoms of the tubes are open. You stuff the toothpaste in and then crimp the bottom shut."

"Oh," I said, much relieved.

My brother James says I'm the only person he knows who would buy 7,200 tubes without stopping to figure out how I was going to get the toothpaste inside.

Even though the toothpaste didn't have to go in the top, it wasn't easy filling the tubes. The bottom opening wasn't as big as on the jars we had been using, and we got a lot of toothpaste on the outside of the tube.

Josie was complaining one day that there must be some easier way of filling tubes than packing the paste in with the end of a spoon. "Isn't there some kind of machine for filling tubes?" she asked Rufus.

"There must be," Rufus said. "I wonder if we could make one."

"We don't even know what one looks like," I said.

"I bet it looks something like this." Rufus got a pencil and started to draw a machine.

"The main part would be a big metal bowl," he said. "Maybe ten, twenty, or thirty feet across the top. So you could mix up ten, twenty, or thirty tons of toothpaste at a time. Bicarb costs a lot less by the ton than by the pound."

Rufus studied the big bowl he had drawn. "The bowl would have a lot of little holes in the bottom," he said. "There would be little hoses running out of the holes.

"How it would work," he explained, "is you'd stick an empty tube at the end of each little hose. Then you'd put a round sheet of metal over the toothpaste mixture. When you pressed down on the metal sheet, the paste would be squeezed into the tubes. Or you could use steam pressure to force the paste down into the tube. You'd have to have a boiler to build up the steam."

As Rufus kept adding parts to the machine, I felt a little discouraged. The machine sounded more complicated than a car motor. And if you've ever looked under the hood of a car, you know that's already too complicated.

Though Rufus was very good at figuring out how to make things, I really didn't think he could make a toothpaste machine. And as it was my idea to put the toothpaste in tubes, I felt responsible for finding an easier way of doing it.

I was sitting in the laundry room one afternoon, staring at one of the cartons the tubes were packed in. I noticed the name of the company that had ordered the tubes from the Perfect Packaging Company. The carton was addressed to Happy Lips Lotion Company, 29 Cuyahoga Avenue, Cleveland, Ohio.

The Happy Lips Lotion Company had gone bankrupt. But before they did, they must have had some kind of machine for filling those 50 gross of tubes.

I looked up Cuyahoga Avenue on a map of Cleveland and rode my bike down there the next day. What I found at 29 Cuyahoga was a small brick factory building. It looked run-down. A sign on the front said FOR RENT—and gave a telephone number.

I walked around the building, trying to look in the windows. But the panes were covered with soot.

I tried the front door of the building. It was locked.

I noticed a man sitting on a bench outside the factory watching me. I wondered if he thought I was trying to break into the building.

I walked a little away from the building and stood there looking it over for a minute—trying to look as if maybe I was thinking of renting it. I even took out a pencil and wrote down the telephone number on the FOR RENT sign.

The man kept watching me as I walked back to my bike. There isn't any law about looking at a building that is for rent. But I thought maybe I should leave.

Before I could get on my bike, the man got up and walked toward me. He was about six feet tall with big shoulders and big hands, and he was carrying a wrench about three feet long.

"Can I help you?" he asked.

"No, thank you," I said. "I'm just looking."

Then I felt silly. I had sounded like my mother in a department store when she isn't really going to buy anything. I felt I had to explain a little more.

"For a machine," I said. "I have this friend who needs a certain kind of machine."

Which I realized sounded even worse. So then I really had to explain. "A machine for filling tooth-paste tubes," I said.

"Yeah?" the man said, and his face lit up as if I'd told him I was on the track of some buried treasure.

"Well, you see, my friend has all these toothpaste tubes," I said. "Over seven thousand of them . . ."

Now that did sound crazy. If you knew about Rufus, it made sense. But if you didn't, it sounded like saying, "I have this friend who has seven thousand banana peels." Or seven thousand refrigerator doors. I mean, what would a normal person be doing with things like that?

"As a matter of fact, *I* gave them to him," I said, hoping I didn't *look* like a crazy person, even if I sounded like one.

"Toothpaste tubes, you said?"

I pulled a sample tube out of my pocket.

"They're like this," I said.

"Oh, sure," the man said. "That's a number five aluminum round-end with round-knurl cap."

"It *is?*" I said.

"Good tube," the man said. "No problem. Bet I've filled a million of them."

"You *have?*" I said. "Are you in the toothpaste business?"

"Right now I'm unemployed," the man said. "But your friend—is *he* in the toothpaste business?"

And that's how I met Hector. Hector was a mechanic who used to work for the Happy Lips Lotion Company. He'd been out of work ever since Happy Lips went bankrupt.

And he'd been hanging around the factory on Cuyahoga Avenue, hoping that whoever rented the plant might need a mechanic to take care of the machinery.

"You mean there's a tube-filling machine still in there?" I asked.

"*Is* there!" Hector said. "It's the most beautiful piece of machinery you ever saw. I practically designed it myself. Would you like to see it?"

Hector and the Happy Lips Plant

The amazing thing about the tube-filling machine was that it looked so much the way Rufus had imagined it would look. I showed Hector Rufus's drawing. Hector seemed to understand it right away.

"He'd need a gear wheel here—and a two-inch pipe feeding in here," Hector said. "The pressure chamber wouldn't have to be so big, but he's got the right idea."

The tube-filling machine was the biggest piece of equipment in the plant. Then there were conveyor belts that carried the tubes to tables where they could be packed for shipping. And there were storage bins for the stuff Happy Lips had used to make lip lotion.

As the plant had looked run-down from the outside, I was surprised at how neat everything was inside. The floors were swept, and the tube-filling machine looked as if someone had been polishing it every day.

Hector said that when a company went bankrupt, it usually sold all its special equipment to help pay its bills. But the Happy Lips Company owed the owner of the building so much rent that they had to leave him the tube-filling machine in place of the rent.

The owner thought it might be easier to rent the plant with all that good equipment in it. But the place had been empty for six months. And the owner, Hector said, was talking now about ripping out the tube-filling machine and selling it for scrap metal.

"That would be a crime," Hector said, "to destroy a beautiful machine like that. It would be a waste." Hector's like Rufus about not wanting to waste anything.

Machines don't usually send me. But I could see how Hector felt about this one. It reminded me a little of that big piece of sculpture the Cleveland Museum had in the entranceway the last time I was there.

The reason the tube-filling machine was in such beautiful condition was that Hector had a key to the place. He came by a couple of times a week to see if the machine needed oiling or anything.

Hector wanted it to be in perfect condition—ready to go on a day's notice, in case somebody came along to rent the place.

The owner of the building was paying Hector a little to keep an eye on the plant. But Hector said it wasn't enough to live on, as he had five kids. He was almost broke, and his wife was bugging him to go into some other line of work.

"I tell her that would be a waste," he said, "being I'm such a good mechanic. I know more about that machine than any mechanic in the United States. On account of my having practically built it and made a lot of improvements on it.

"If your friend rented the place and hired me to look after the machinery," Hector said, "we could be in full production tomorrow. No problem."

I could picture it. The tube machine filled with toothpaste, humming away, squeezing out thousands of tubes of toothpaste every hour. Hector working the machine, and Rufus and I and the other stockholders packing Toothpaste and mailing it out to customers all over the United States. I couldn't wait to get home to tell Rufus.

Hector said, "I think the rent's only about three hundred a month."

"Rent?" I said. "Oh."

That brought me down to earth. Three hundred seemed like a lot. Of course, I realized you couldn't expect to get a factory with the machinery in it for nothing. And you certainly couldn't fit a machine like that into our laundry room.

Then there was Hector, too. I didn't think we could run the machine without him. And Rufus couldn't ask Hector to work like his friends—for a share of the profits at the end of the year. Not when he was broke and had five kids to feed.

"And how much would *you* cost, Hector?" I asked.

"I was getting nine thousand from Happy Lips," Hector said. "I got to make at least nine thousand dollars a year to pay my bills."

So that would be $9,000, plus the rent. That

might be okay if Rufus already had the profits from the first year of being in business. But, of course, he didn't.

Then again, if Rufus could figure out a plan for making millions, maybe he could think of some way to get only a few thousand dollars.

I told Hector I would have to talk it over with my friend.

"You bring him here," he said. "I'll show him how everything works."

I said I'd bring Rufus the next day.

"Just one question," Hector said, as I was getting on my bike. "About Mr. Rufus. Would he discriminate?"

"What do you mean?" I asked.

"I mean about hiring me," Hector said. "On account of I'm black."

"Oh," I said. "Well, Rufus is, too."

"He *is?*" Hector said.

"More and more people you meet are," I said.

"I guess you're right," he said. "Well, I'm glad to have met you, too."

Riding home, I didn't know whether I'd done

the right thing or not in going down to 29 Cuyahoga Avenue. I began to worry that maybe I'd gotten Hector's hopes up too much.

My father's always saying that one thing leads to another. It certainly does. I start out to buy a friend a birthday present, and I end up trying to get him a factory to go with it and to find a job for a man with five kids.

I never had that kind of problem in Fairhaven, Connecticut.

CHAPTER

14

The Trouble with Adults

Rufus did think I was a little out of my mind when I told him I had found him not only a toothpaste machine but a whole factory and mechanic to go with it. And he did wonder if we couldn't somehow get to use the machine without hiring Hector as well.

I tried to explain that Hector and the machine seemed to belong together. And that I didn't think we could get one without the other.

As soon as he met Hector, Rufus understood. And as soon as Hector heard the details of Rufus's plan for keeping the price of Toothpaste low and profits high at the same time, he thought it was a beautiful idea.

"That Happy Lips Lotion," Hector said, "a dollar ninety-eight a tube! Nothing in it but a little lanolin and a speck of perfume to make it smell nice. Maybe it made your lips feel nice. But it sure was a high-priced way to feel nice."

Hector explained everything about the machine to Rufus. How many tubes it could fill in an hour. How many helpers Hector would need to turn out so many tubes. He and Rufus were talking as if it were all settled that Rufus was going to rent the plant.

"It would be a shame not to," Rufus said on the way home. "We know we've got a good idea. We've got all those tubes. Now the machine. *And* Hector. All we need is a little money."

"Quite a lot, Rufus," I said.

"So how much?" Rufus said. "Let's see—nine thousand for Hector, thirty-six hundred for rent, and maybe a little more—in case we have to buy some more tubes—I guess we'll need about fifteen thousand dollars."

"How are you going to get fifteen thousand dollars?" I asked. "Just walk in a bank and ask for it?"

"Hey!" Rufus said. "Why not? Isn't that what other people do?"

"A stickup, you mean?" I said.

"No, no," Rufus said. "I mean the way other businessmen do. The *big* businessmen."

What Rufus decided to do was to go to Everybody's Friendly Savings & Loan and borrow some money. Everybody's Friendly Savings & Loan was the sponsor of *The Joe Smiley Show*.

Five times every night, this friendly vice president Seymour Perkell interrupted the show to do a commercial telling how friendly Everybody's Friendly Savings & Loan was about lending everybody money. To buy a car. Or start a business. And how they liked to encourage young businessmen who were starting businesses in the neighborhood. And how they believed in people, and how people were their business.

The way Mr. Perkell made it sound, Everybody's Friendly Savings & Loan was dying to lend everybody money. So Rufus called up the office and asked for an appointment with Mr. Perkell.

When we got to the office, the lady at the front desk didn't want to let us see Mr. Perkell. She said he had an appointment at four o'clock.

Rufus said. "So do I. My name is Rufus

Mayflower, and Mr. Perkell's four o'clock appointment is with me."

The lady looked at an appointment calendar on
her desk and said, "*Oh, you're* Mr. Mayflower?" I
don't think she expected Mr. Mayflower to look so
young.

She called in to Mr. Perkell's office to tell him,
"Mr. Perkell, there is a *young* man here to see
you—and there is a *young* lady with him."

I didn't care for the way she said *young*, as if
Rufus and I were about four years old. But Rufus
walked into Mr. Perkell's office as if he'd been bor-
rowing money all his life.

Mr. Perkell looked more tired than he did on
TV and not as friendly. But he warmed up a little
when I told him we saw him every night on the *Joe
Smiley* commercial and that he was very good.

"Ah," he said. "And what can I do for you?"

"You can lend me some money for a business
I'm starting," Rufus said.

"Rufus was on *The Joe Smiley Show* a couple of
weeks ago," I said, as Mr. Perkell looked as if he
needed a little more warming up. "Joe Smiley says

that he got a lot of listener response to that show, and Rufus got orders for six hundred and eighty-nine jars of Toothpaste."

"Ah," Mr. Perkell said to Rufus. "So that's where I've seen you. You're the boy who makes toothpaste."

"Yes," Rufus said. He explained to Mr. Perkell that he now had 7,200 toothpaste tubes, a machine for filling them, and a man who knew how to run the machine. And that all he needed to get into production was about $15,000. Which he could easily pay back in a year, because within one year he could easily be selling 250 million tubes of Toothpaste. Rufus had written out on a piece of paper all the facts about the population of the United States and the 1¢ profit.

Mr. Perkell went over Rufus's figures carefully. He couldn't find anything wrong with them.

"You have a very good idea," Mr. Perkell said. "And you have figured everything out in a very businesslike way."

"So can you lend me the money today?" Rufus asked.

Mr. Perkell looked unhappy. "I'm afraid I can't lend you the money at all," he said.

"How come?" Rufus said. "I thought you lent money to everybody."

"Well, not exactly *everybody*," Mr. Perkell said. "Not exactly," it turned out, meant "not kids."

The trouble with adults is that they never believe kids can do something even when they have good ideas.

Mr. Perkell admitted that if a responsible adult with a regular job and no debts came to ask for a loan with the *same* idea Rufus had, he'd probably get the money.

"I hope you understand," Mr. Perkell said. "It's nothing against you personally. It's just that you're—ah, *young*."

"In your commercial, it says you encourage young businessmen," Rufus said.

That stopped Mr. Perkell for a minute. Then he said, "Well, yes, we do—but what business experience have you had?"

"Rufus has sold over a thousand jars of Toothpaste in four weeks," I said.

"Ah," Mr. Perkell said. "And are you Mr. Mayflower's partner in business?"

"She is a stockholder," Rufus said.

Which I thought was a *very* businesslike way to end the meeting.

Having made the point about adults never believing kids can do anything, I have to take that back. Or, at least, to admit there are exceptions. Hector, for example.

What Rufus really felt bad about the afternoon we left Mr. Perkell's office was Hector. We'd have to tell him that we couldn't get the money.

"It doesn't matter about us," Rufus said. "We can still make Toothpaste in the laundry room. Enough for our friends and families. But Hector really needs a job."

And Hector was mad when we told him. Furious.

"Stupid! Stupid! Stupid!" Hector said, stomping around the lot outside the factory. He was so mad he picked up a rock and heaved it against the wall of the factory.

I thought at first he meant Rufus was stupid. Or that *he* was stupid for believing Rufus could start a business. But he meant Mr. Perkell!

"Because you had a good idea, kid," he said to Rufus. "A million-dollar idea. Just because you're only twelve years old doesn't mean it isn't a good idea. I've been in this business, and I can tell a good idea. And we've got the perfect machine for it. It's stupid to let that perfectly good machine stand there. It's a waste. It's a crime. It's stupid."

"Hey!" Rufus suddenly brightened up as if he had a ten-million-dollar idea. "Hector," he said, "I believe you. I believe you would lend me the money—if you *had* the money, that is."

"Believe me, I would," Hector said.

"Great!" Rufus said. "Then it's easy. All we've got to do, Hector, is for *you* to go to Mr. Perkell and ask him to lend you fifteen thousand dollars to invest in a business."

"*Me!*" Hector said.

"*You,*" Rufus said.

Rufus turned to me. "Didn't Mr. Perkell say that if I were a responsible adult with a regular job and no debts, he would lend me the money?"

"That's what he said," I said.

"And you're a responsible adult, Hector!" Rufus said.

"Yeah," Hector said, "except I don't have a regular job. So how could I pay the money back?"

"*Simple,*" Rufus said. "I am going to hire you as manager of the toothpaste factory. The money you borrow to invest in the business, I can use to pay your first year's salary. And to pay the rent. And to buy some more toothpaste tubes, which we will probably need."

Hector scratched his head. "You mean I'm going to borrow the money? And I'm going to invest it in your business? So you can use it to pay me?"

"Right," Rufus said. "But that's not *all*. For the fifteen thousand you invest in the business, I will give you a hundred and fifty shares of stock in the company. At the end of the year, you will get part of the profits of the company because you will be a major stockholder."

"A major stockholder?" Hector said.

Rufus explained to Hector about the stock.

That if Hector owned 150 shares of the stock, he'd own 15 percent of the business. And that if the company did make a $2.5 million profit, he'd get 15 percent of that.

"Which would come to three hundred and seventy-five thousand dollars," Rufus said. "That's *more than enough* to pay back the fifteen thousand to the Everybody's Friendly Savings & Loan."

"You sure you got that figured right, Rufus?" Hector said.

I told Hector we had checked out stockholders' profits in our math class. The whole class worked on it and Mr. Conti checked the answers.

"Do it, Hector!" I said. "Go ask Mr. Perkell for the money."

"You mean I'd *own* part of the business?" Hector said.

"Yep," Rufus said. "And get paid every week, too."

"Oh, that would be beautiful," Hector said. "Beautiful. There's just one question. Does this Mr. Perkell discriminate?"

I knew what Hector meant.

"As far as I know, just against kids," Rufus said.

A year later, Hector said when he was being interviewed about Rufus on *The Joe Smiley Show:*

Maybe anybody can make toothpaste in his own kitchen. But speaking for myself, all I know is one day I'm a mechanic out of work, and the next day I'm a general manager and major stockholder. And that takes genius.

Hector believed Rufus was a genius from the beginning. When Mr. Perkell okayed the business loan to Hector, Hector handed the $15,000 check straight to Rufus. Rufus put the money in a bank account and wrote Hector a check for his first month's salary.

My father claims that one of the best proofs of Rufus's genius was his hiring Hector to run the toothpaste factory.

"Of course," I have to remind my father, "*I* was the one who discovered Hector."

The nice thing about Rufus is that *he* always does remember that it was me who found Hector *and* the toothpaste machine.

Toothpaste 1. That's what the kids at school called our math class the second term of the year. After Rufus really got into the toothpaste business, Mr. Conti picked up several new toothpaste problems every week.

Since the class seemed to like working on Rufus's toothpaste problems better than those Mr. Conti thought up, Mr. Conti decided we might as well all concentrate on the toothpaste business. By the end of the term, half the class were stockholders in the company. Even Mr. Conti sometimes came down to the factory on Saturday to see how things were going.

Hector could hardly believe he was bossing around a math teacher. Hector never finished high school.

What was really cool about Toothpaste 1 was that Mr. Conti asked Rufus and me to make up the final exam for the class. That meant Rufus and I would know all the right answers before the test.

Mr. Conti told the class that this was *not* an unfair advantage. He said thinking up the right problems to be answered is often harder than thinking up the right answers.

In case you're not crazy about math, maybe I'd better explain about some of the toothpaste problems we worked on in class. As I mentioned before, math isn't my favorite subject. But I think everybody should take a course in toothpaste.

Rufus had the sensible idea of getting the toothpaste straight to the person who wanted to use it. In Toothpaste 1, we figured out the cheapest way of doing this.

We discovered that it would cost Rufus about 10¢ a tube to mail the toothpaste to a customer. But if he mailed twelve tubes at once, the postage would come to only 5¢ to 9¢ a tube, depending on how far we were mailing it. Say an average cost of 7¢ a tube.

That gave Rufus the idea that he should sell a customer a year's supply of toothpaste at a time to save them money on postage. Since a year's supply of our toothpaste didn't cost much more than one tube of the brands you see in stores, our customers could afford to order twelve tubes at once.

Sometimes Rufus likes to talk about the "good old days" when he was putting his toothpaste in jars by hand and delivering it in person on his bike. In those "good old days" Rufus could sell toothpaste for 3¢—and still make a profit. When he got into big business, he had to charge 15¢.

Not that Rufus was taking a bigger profit. But there were a few other expenses, such as 7¢ for postage and 4¢ for tubes.

Once we'd filled the tubes I got at the auction, we had to buy tubes, like any other toothpaste business. It bothered Rufus that a tube should cost more than the stuff that went in it. But he didn't have time that year to get into making his own tubes.

Actually the cost of the stuff that went *into* the paste went down (from 2¢ to 1¢) once Rufus started buying the ingredients by the ton. But at the same time he had to add 1¢ to the cost of making the paste for the extra expense of the rent and electricity at the plant—and Hector's pay.

Chapter 16

There was another 1¢ cost that we didn't have when we were making Toothpaste in my laundry. Advertising.

Rufus said that was one cost we shouldn't try to cut down on too much. After all, we couldn't get as many as one out of ten people in the country to switch to Toothpaste unless they *knew* about Toothpaste.

At first, the only TV advertising we could afford was on local stations. We would advertise one week on a Detroit station and the next in San Diego or Seattle, and the word got around.

So these were our expenses per tube:

for paste	1¢
for tubes	4¢
for plant, packaging, Hector, etc.	1¢
for advertising	1¢
TOTAL COST OF TOOTHPASTE	7¢
plus profit	1¢
plus postage	7¢
RUFUS'S PRICE PER TUBE	15¢

◆ ◆ ◆

After selling toothpaste for 3¢, 15¢ always seemed a high price to Rufus. He kept telling people in our commercials that if they wanted to make their own at home and save the postage, he would send them the recipe. Quite a few people did write in for the recipe.

Rufus did everything he could to keep the cost of Toothpaste low. In his commercials, he told people who wanted to order Toothpaste to print their names and addresses on postcards. We cut off the addresses and pasted them on the mailing cartons so we didn't have to waste time addressing orders.

Also, we used only one mailing carton for twelve tubes. We didn't put each tube in separate boxes which would just have to be thrown away.

Do you know how many tons of cardboard it takes to make boxes for 250 million tubes of toothpaste? You can weigh one toothpaste box and figure it out. That's the kind of problem we worked on in Toothpaste 1.

17

The Absolutely Honest Commercial

I know commercials are supposed to be boring. But I liked making the commercials for Toothpaste more than any other part of the business.

It was like making movies. In fact, that's what it was.

Rufus knew a kid named Lee Lu who had a movie camera. Lee Lu had made a complete movie about cockroaches that was so good it was shown in all the Cleveland schools.

Rufus asked Lee Lu if he would help us make some commercials we could show on TV. The first one we made with Lee Lu showed Rufus talking about the toothpaste the way he did on *The Joe Smiley Show*. Telling people Toothpaste was just plain toothpaste—inexpensive to make and inexpensive to buy.

We'd start off with Rufus telling a story about his Grandma Mayflower. Rufus had some snapshots of his grandmother that Lee Lu used between shots of Rufus talking about Toothpaste.

Though we were getting good results with these commercials, Rufus got a letter one day from a girl in Boston. She asked how come the Toothpaste commercials always showed a *boy* talking about the toothpaste. She said that was "discrimination."

Rufus said maybe she was right. He didn't want people to think Toothpaste was just for boys—or men. He had Josie and Clem go through a week's orders to see if more of them were from males than females. They were.

So then we made a commercial with me in it. I'd never been in a movie and thought I would be nervous in front of a camera. But Lee Lu said I didn't have to act, just be natural, and he'd do the rest.

"Trust me," he said. "Remember how good those cockroaches came out?"

I don't know if I came out as natural as the cockroaches. My brother James said I was funny. Which I didn't think I was. My father said not to worry if I was, as that wouldn't hurt sales.

My mother was more tactful. She said I was

"surprisingly photogenic." By which she meant I looked better in the movie than I do in real life. Which is probably true. My freckles hardly show on TV.

In my commercial, I explained why Toothpaste was mailed to customers in a plain cardboard box with no jazzy color printing on it. That was because it kept the cost low.

Clem and Josie were in another commercial. They showed how we cut the names and addresses of our customers off the postcards they sent us and pasted them right on the plain cardboard boxes. That way we didn't have to pay anybody to address orders.

But our best commercial, I thought, was one of Hector. We made a one-minute movie of Hector explaining how the toothpaste machine worked. In that commercial Hector keeps ducking out of the way of the camera to be sure everybody gets a good view of the machine. *That* is a funny commercial.

Lee Lu's movies of all of us telling about Toothpaste were so good that a lot of kids at school wanted to come to work in the plant so they could be in one of the movies.

Every time we ran one of our commercials on a new station, we got a lot of new customers. Since our customers were ordering a year's supply of Toothpaste at a time, we didn't have to advertise to the same people every week. We could run a commercial on a Denver, Colorado, station once, and people who saw it would send in a year's order.

We were doing all right just showing our commercials on local TV stations around the country. You can imagine what happened when one of the big networks ran our four best commercials one night *for free*.

Morton McCallister on his evening news show had a report on what he called "The Absolutely Honest Commercial." He reported that people who hated commercials had discovered one commercial they loved to watch—because it was "absolutely honest."

Morton McCallister showed four of our commercials: one with Rufus talking, one with me, one with Clem and Josie, and the one of Hector at the plant. After each commercial Morton McCallister showed how people in different parts of the country reacted.

He showed a lady in Miami Beach, a family in Cedar Rapids, Iowa, some college kids in a diner, and some migrant workers in California.

After he showed examples of our commercials, Morton McCallister said in The Sum-Up he does every night at the end of the show:

And so to sum up: To a nation weary of wondrous claims for costly creations of sometimes dubious merit, the manufacturers of Toothpaste have been demonstrating that honesty may be the best policy after all.

The Toothpaste "commercials"—if they can be called that—simply tell us what's in Toothpaste and how much it costs. The advertising executives in their glittering headquarters along Madison Avenue do not understand why these commercials, filmed by Cleveland schoolchildren, should be selling more toothpaste than their very expensive, clever, and sophisticated productions.

Perhaps it is that these Toothpaste commer-

cials shine like a good deed in a naughty world, refresh like a fresh breeze across polluted airwaves, and provoke us all to wonder whether the best things in life—if not absolutely free—might not be simpler and less expensive than they usually are.

Isn't that beautiful?

I thought it was so beautiful I memorized it to recite in a class where we had to give part of a famous speech like the Gettysburg Address or "Ask Not What Your Country Can Do for You."

Millions of people who might have missed our commercials on local stations saw them on Morton McCallister's news show. Naturally Rufus got thousands of new orders.

Several big toothpaste companies were furious with Morton McCallister. They said it was absolutely unfair to give all that free advertising to one company.

Morton McCallister replied that an absolutely honest commercial was news, not advertising. But three of the companies, Sparkle, Dazzle, and Brite, demanded equal time on his news program.

The president of the network got nervous that Sparkle and Dazzle and Brite might not advertise on his network anymore. He told Morton McCallister that he would have to give them equal time.

So Morton McCallister on his next news show explained that Sparkle and Dazzle and Brite felt it wasn't fair to show our absolutely honest commercials without showing theirs, too. And to be absolutely fair, Morton McCallister said that he was going to show three examples—one from each of the companies—of commercials that *weren't* absolutely honest.

Well, when people saw three of those in a row, it really turned them off. And Rufus got millions more orders. Which wasn't what Sparkle and Dazzle and Brite had in mind at all.

"THE BEST BUY IN TOOTHPASTE IS TOOTHPASTE."

That was the headline on the May issue of *Consumer's Friend* last year. It was that headline that started the price war.

Consumer's Friend is a magazine that tests products and tells readers which brands are the best to buy. Last spring they tested toothpaste and reported that Rufus's toothpaste was "the best buy."

"The best buy" wasn't purely a matter of price. *Consumer's Friend* rated toothpastes for performance, safety, and taste, as well as price. They tested how well the toothpaste cleaned your teeth and whether there were any harmful ingredients in the toothpaste.

Consumer's Friend discovered that one of the most expensive brands could be very irritating to your mouth and another could scratch the enamel on your teeth.

When the *Consumer's Friend* report came out, Rufus started getting so many more orders that Hector almost had a nervous breakdown. He had to order two new toothpaste machines and hire fourteen people full-time to help fill the orders.

Rufus was making enough money by then to pay for the extra equipment and workers, but the factory was getting crowded.

Fortunately, the price war didn't start until June, about the time school let out. So Rufus and I and all the kids who owned stock in the company could spend a lot more time helping Hector.

When thousands of people overnight started switching to Toothpaste, the manufacturers of name brands started cutting their prices. The first week of the price war, the Cut-Rate Drugstore near us had Sparkle for 69¢, Dazzle for 63¢, and Brite for 59¢.

The next week Sparkle was down to 58¢, Dazzle to 57¢, and Brite down to 53¢. Every day another company slashed its price, trying to win back customers. Some brands were down to 39¢. Several companies folded.

Every time a company folded, Rufus got more orders. And with a lot of empty toothpaste factories around, Hector was able to rent a few of these temporarily to pack the orders that were piling up at 29 Cuyahoga Avenue.

Since the price of Toothpaste was already so low, the price war didn't hurt our business at all. In fact, it helped by waking up a lot of people to how much they had been paying for toothpaste.

When a customer switched from Dazzle to Brite, Dazzle lost one sale. But if a customer switched from Dazzle to Toothpaste, Dazzle lost *twelve* sales, because our orders were for a year's supply at a time. Once a customer switched to Toothpaste, he wasn't going to be shopping for toothpaste for a whole year.

The last week of school, we spent most of the time in Mr. Conti's class keeping track of the price war. Someone wrote up the latest figures on the chalkboard every day:

DAZZLE *down* 2 (cents)	TOOTHPASTE *up* 1,999 (sales)
SPARKLE *down* 3	TOOTHPASTE *up* 21,701
BRITE *down* 4	TOOTHPASTE *up* 53,422
SENSATION *bankrupt*	TOOTHPASTE *up* 100,001

◆ ◆ ◆

The more the big brands slashed their prices, the faster Toothpaste increased its sales. And suddenly there was my friend Rufus on the cover of *Business Month* as "Businessman of the Year."

The week that Sparkle cut its price to 39¢ and there were rumors that Dazzle was folding, Rufus got a telegram. It was an invitation to meet with major representatives of the toothpaste industry to discuss the health of the industry.

The major representatives turned out to be the three guys Hector calls Sparkle, Dazzle, and Brite. They were the presidents of the companies that make those brands.

Sparkle was George Gorden Westingshed III, of Westingshed Pharmaceuticals, Inc.

Dazzle was Ron Medicine, of Medicine Pharmaceuticals, Ltd.

And Brite was Mel Melliphone, of Melifluous Pharmaceuticals, Paper Products, Cereals & Aerospace Industries, Inc.

In the first months of the price war, Sparkle, Dazzle, and Brite had been mainly trying to kill off each other. Then they realized that Rufus was the one they had to get.

A Movie Script by Mac Kinstrey

The price war gave me an idea for my life career. I think I may write movie scripts.

As Morton McCallister pointed out, the reason people liked our commercials was that they were true. And I think movies might be better if they were more true-to-life.

I have an idea for my first script. It will be called *The Toothpaste War* and is based on real life. Here is a rough outline of how it would go:

The movie is about this kid named Ray Flower who starts a toothpaste business. He is so successful that it looks like he is going to put all the big toothpaste companies out of business. The movie starts with a price war.
Scene 1: Cut-Rate Drugstore
Camera: Close-up of sign in window.

SHINE TOOTHPASTE — REGULARLY 79¢
SLASHED TO 69¢

Camera: Cuts to another sign.

SMILE SLASHED TO 68¢

Camera: Cuts to

SENSATION SLASHED TO 67¢

While this price war in the drugstore window is going on, the movie credits fade in:

THE TOOTHPASTE WAR

Script by Mac Kinstrey

Cameraman: Lee Lu

And so on . . .

Then we cut to Scene 2:

A top-secret meeting in the biggest suite on the top floor of a ritzy hotel in downtown Cleveland. There is a big table in the room, loaded with turkey sandwiches, champagne, and three bottles of cream soda. The main characters in this scene are:

RAY: a nice-looking boy about five feet tall with black curly hair. He wears a blue sweater.

VICTOR: a strong-looking man about six and a half feet tall with black curly hair. He wears overalls.

MAC: a girl; four-foot-eleven, with freckles and straight brown hair. Not beautiful, but she looks trustworthy. (*I haven't decided yet what she will wear.*)

SHARKLE, SNAZZLE, and SLYTE: three middle-aged men. SHARKLE is bald, and SNAZZLE and SLYTE are almost bald. SHARKLE looks mean, SNAZZLE looks greedy, and SLYTE looks sly. They wear expensive business suits.

(*Lee Lu can shoot this scene either with very bright lights that show up the true characters of* SHARKLE, SNAZZLE, *and* SLYTE, *or with very dim lights that make them look sinister and as if they have something to hide. I'm not sure which would be best.*)

What happens in this scene is that SHARKLE, SNAZZLE, *and* SLYTE *try to make a deal with* RAY FLOWER. *The conversation goes something like this:*

SHARKLE: We realize, Mr. Flower, that starting out in a small way, you had to keep your prices low until your product was well known.

SNAZZLE: But now that you are a leader in the market, you, of course, have the same interest we do in keeping profits high.

SLYTE: Until this terrible price war, we were keeping things peaceful in the toothpaste business.

SHARKLE: And profits high.

SNAZZLE: None of us were selling toothpaste for less than seventy-nine cents for the economy-size tube.

SLYTE: Except for special sales.

SHARKLE: Three times a year.

SNAZZLE: Three times when we lowered prices by three cents for three days.

SLYTE: To encourage customers.

SHARKLE: Sharkle runs a special in March.

SNAZZLE: Snazzle runs a special in June.

SLYTE: Slyte runs a special in October.

SHARKLE: We all take a turn.

SNAZZLE: And you could run your special in January, Mr. Flower.

Chapter 19

RAY: If I lowered my price by three cents, my company would go broke. I make only one cent a tube.

SHARKLE: But that's so silly.

SNAZZLE: If you became a member of our little group, you could sell your toothpaste for seventy-nine cents.

RAY: I think seventy-nine cents is too much for toothpaste.

SHARKLE: Perhaps we could all agree on a *slightly* lower price.

RAY: Like fifteen cents?

Sound: SNAZZLE *and* SLYTE *laughing nervously.*

SHARKLE: You must be kidding, Mr. Flower.

RAY: What do you think, Victor?

VICTOR: I think they're trying to make a deal with you, kid.

RAY: What do you think, Mac?

MAC: Let's get out of here, Ray.

Sound: Hotel door being busted down.

Camera: Pans to three FBI MEN *crashing in.*

1ST FBI MAN: Nobody move.

2ND FBI MAN: This room is bugged.

3RD FBI MAN: You guys are under arrest.

Camera: Close-up of handcuffs on SHARKLE, SNAZZLE, *and* SLYTE

1ST FBI MAN: Organized Crime is holding a meeting in the next room.

2ND FBI MAN: We were just getting our equipment set up.

3RD FBI MAN: And we happened to hear your conversation.

SHARKLE: We were just discussing the health of the toothpaste business.

1ST FBI MAN: Price-fixing is a federal crime.

SNAZZLE: But we didn't get anything fixed.

3RD FBI MAN: Conspiracy to fix is also a crime.

SLYTE: Wiretapping is against the law.

1ST FBI MAN: We'll see about that.

(FBI MEN *exit, dragging* SHARKLE, SNAZZLE, *and* SLYTE)

VICTOR: We might as well eat the turkey sandwiches.

Scene 3 all takes place in a telephone booth. SHARKLE, SNAZZLE, *and* SLYTE *are out on bail. Their trial hasn't come up yet, and they are still plotting to get* RAY FLOWER. *Since* RAY *won't agree to their price-fixing, they try to buy up his company.*
Camera: Close-up of SHARKLE *in a telephone booth on a dark street corner.*

SHARKLE: I'm making you an offer on your five hundred and one shares of stock. A thousand bucks a share. It was worth only a hundred bucks a share when you started.

RAY'S VOICE: (On phone) No thanks.

Camera: Close-up of SNAZZLE *in booth.*

SNAZZLE: Two thousand dollars a share for every share you own. You could be a rich man.

VICTOR'S VOICE: (On phone) No thanks. I'd rather be part owner of the company.

Camera: Close-up of SLYTE.

SLYTE:	What would you say to three thousand bucks a share for your shares of stock?
MAC'S VOICE:	Goodbye.

That's as far as I've gone on the script. I don't know whether the movie will end with Sharkle, Snazzle, and Slyte in jail or not. Because the trials of Sparkle, Dazzle, and Brite haven't taken place yet. These things take a long time.

I could end the movie with Joey the Bomb blowing up the plant on Cuyahoga Avenue. My father, though, says that was such a crazy-way-out thing to happen that if I put it in the script, the movie won't seem very true-to-life.

I'm tempted to put Joey the Bomb in the movie anyway. He's more likeable than Sparkle, Dazzle, and Brite.

Also, Joey was hired to blow up the plant. It wasn't his idea.

Joey didn't have any grudge against Rufus personally. And *he personally* decided to get Rufus and me and Hector out of the plant before he set off the bomb.

Joey *is* in jail now. It was definitely proved that he was the bomber, though the police haven't caught up with the guy who hired him.

All the police know is that the guy who hired Joey is with Organized Crime. That was what the meeting in the next room of the hotel was about.

It seems Organized Crime owns a lot of companies, including toothpaste factories. When someone cuts in on their business, they don't bother with price-fixing deals.

Rufus and I have gone to see Joey the Bomb in jail a couple of times. We feel grateful to him for saving our lives. He might not be in jail if we hadn't been alive to identify him when the cops nabbed him.

Hector wouldn't go with us to visit Joey. He never will forgive Joey for blowing up the plant.

Although Rufus was planning to rent a bigger plant with a tube-filling machine that could fill ten times as many tubes an hour, Hector was heartbroken about losing the old machine. Even the first year's profits didn't cheer Hector.

Rufus didn't sell quite the 250 million tubes he'd planned to sell in his first year of business. But he came close. The company's profits were a little over $2 million. Even after dividing up 49 percent of the profits among the other stockholders, Rufus still had over a million dollars.

The plant getting bombed turned out to be the least of Rufus's problems. His real headaches started when Sparkle, Dazzle, and Brite, plus a lot of other people, began calling up our stockholders, trying to buy up stock in the company.

Most of the kids who owned stock realized they had a good thing and wouldn't sell. But a couple of the kids wanted to make some quick money, and they agreed to sell their shares. When they turned their stock certificates over to the stock buyers, the buyers flipped—because the certificates looked to them like play money.

My father says that's all stock certificates are anyway. But the stock buyers still flipped.

We all knew Rufus's stock certificates came from his Stock Market game. But it seems that if you're in real business, you're supposed to have real certificates. And lawyers okaying how the company is set up. And records for the government. There are a lot of Rules & Regulations we didn't know about.

And the first thing we did know about them was a headline in the *Cleveland Plain Dealer:* "BOY FINANCIAL WIZARD ACCUSED OF FRAUD." Then the *Business Monthly* article: "IS TOOTHPASTE STOCK BOGUS?"

And the second thing we know, there is a

Special Investigation, and it looks as if Rufus may be going to jail along with Sparkle, Dazzle, and Brite. FBI agents come around, wanting to see Rufus's books.

The books they want to see are account books, which show the company's earnings. All Rufus had for books was a spiral notebook in which he jotted the number of orders, what our expenses were, and the profit we made every week.

The FBI was used to businesses that had sets and sets and sets of books. And accountants to explain how they added up business expenses and to send reports to the government. Rufus didn't have any accountants. He just had me checking to see that he hadn't made a mistake in addition.

When the FBI saw Rufus's spiral notebook, they were sure he must have some other books hidden away somewhere. The more the FBI and the Cleveland district attorney and newspaper reporters investigated, the longer the list got of Rules & Regulations Rufus hadn't paid any attention to. This was the only time I ever heard Rufus sound discouraged.

But as things turned out, the point of all these Rules & Regulations was to protect customers and stockholders from fraud. And the Special Investigation proved that Rufus hadn't cheated *anyone*.

Rufus's toothpaste had in it exactly what he said it did. And every stockholder had been paid his fair share of the profits, even if the stock certificates weren't the real thing. So Rufus couldn't be found guilty of fraud. Only of not filling out certain forms in a certain way.

As my father said, "Rufus's only crime was cutting through a lot of red tape. He should be an example to the whole country."

CHAPTER

21

The Board of Directors

As soon as it was clear that Rufus wasn't going to have to go to jail for the rest of his life, Mr. Perkell of the Everybody's Friendly Savings & Loan called Rufus to ask for an appointment with him.

Mr. Perkell told Rufus that he had followed his business career with interest and had been very impressed. And he wanted to give Rufus a little friendly business advice.

Mr. Perkell's advice was that now that Rufus had such a big business, he needed some lawyers and accountants who knew about the Rules & Regulations. Mr. Perkell wanted to offer the legal and financial services of the Everybody's Friendly Savings & Loan.

He also thought Rufus should have a Board of Directors, of which Mr. Perkell would naturally be a member.

Rufus discussed this with all of the stockholders. We decided maybe it was a good idea. What really convinced us was the income tax.

Mr. Conti told Rufus that he would help us figure out the company's income tax. But income tax regulations for business are very complicated. In fact, they're so complicated that Mr. Conti gave up and said we'd have to get an accountant.

So where things are now is that the Everybody's Friendly Savings & Loan is lending us money to build a new Toothpaste plant outside Cleveland. And we have a Board of Directors: Rufus, Mr. Perkell, Mr. Conti, Morton McCallister, Hector, and me. And a lawyer whose name I can't remember.

Hector's on the board because Rufus insisted he knows more about the business than any of us. I'm on it because Mr. Perkell says you have to have a woman on a Board of Directors these days.

Rufus, though, says he voted for me not because of that, but because he trusts me.

The new Toothpaste factory was almost finished when Rufus suddenly decided to retire from the toothpaste business.

"Retire!" I said. "Just when you're making so much money."

"Anybody can make money," Rufus said. "It only takes a little common sense. The fact is that making money isn't too interesting to me. Figuring out how to make the toothpaste was fun. And figuring out how I could make money by charging less, instead of more, was fun. But ever since we figured those things out, it seems as if I've been doing the same thing over and over again."

I couldn't think of a good answer to that.

"I'd rather figure out something new to do," Rufus said.

"But what will happen to the company?" I asked.

"Hector can run it," Rufus said. "He's been running it all along. I just had the idea, so I'm going to sell him my stock. Hector won't sell the business to anyone who wants to make seventy-nine-cent toothpaste."

And right after school closed, Rufus did retire. And he went to North Carolina to spend the summer with his Grandma Mayflower.

He went to North Carolina by bicycle. That's the crazy thing about Rufus. Here he is a millionaire who could jump on a jet plane. But instead he packs a sleeping bag and an extra pair of socks and shirt in his blue saddlebags. And his toothbrush, of course. And sets off on his bike.

I really miss Rufus this summer, though I have a lot of friends in East Cleveland now. All the kids who worked in the toothpaste business with Rufus and me, as well as people we met through the business like Hector and Mr. Perkell and Joe Smiley and Vince. Mr. Perkell even offered me a summer job in the Everybody's Friendly Savings & Loan.

But my father and mother thought I should take a summer vacation, since I worked at the toothpaste factory all last summer, as well as after school for almost two years. And it's not as if I needed the money. At the moment I'm pretty rich myself from being a stockholder in Rufus's company.

So I'm spending this summer reading books and getting rested up for when Rufus gets back from North Carolina. I'm sure he will have figured out some project that's even more fun than just making a million dollars.

Yesterday I got a postcard from Rufus from Nashville, Tennessee. It said:

Could you see if Vince's Army & Navy sells blow-up rafts at least 6' x 12'? And how much would two of them cost? And do they have army-surplus dried soup in 100-pound bags?

I'm on my way to Vince's now. If America hadn't already been discovered, it wouldn't surprise me at all if that was what Rufus had in mind.

A conversation with Jean Merrill, author,
on the thirty-fifth anniversary of
The Toothpaste Millionaire

Q. When did you begin to write?

A. After graduating from college in 1945, I worked for Scholastic Magazines, writing movie and record reviews as well as stories and plays, and doing interviews of people in the news. Around 1950, I became friends with Ronni Solbert, a painter who wanted to illustrate children's books. So I wrote my first children's book, *Henry, the Hand-Painted Mouse*, and she illustrated it. In 1965, I began working for the Bank Street College of Education, helping to plan and edit stories for their Bank Street Readers series, and also writing many of them.

Q. What kind of a schedule do you have when you are writing? Do you know the end when you start a book?

A. When I am on a project I spend most of the day working and am pretty regular about that. I don't always know what the end of a book will be. I was pretty sure Rufus and Kate would succeed in their toothpaste business, but at the start I wasn't sure how they'd do it.

Q. How many books have you published?

A. About thirty, plus a lot of stories and plays for magazines and for Bank Street College's Publications Division. *The Toothpaste Millionaire* was written for Bank Street's Discovery series, which was published by Houghton Mifflin.

Q. What was your inspiration for writing *The Toothpaste Millionaire*?

A. I knew a dentist who practiced in a poor section of New York City. He created a simple toothpaste recipe his patients could make at home. Some friends wanted to start a business to manufacture the toothpaste. I didn't. I wasn't a businessperson.

But when Bank Street asked me to write a novel for the Discovery series, I decided to do it about how schoolkids could create a successful business making inexpensive toothpaste.

Another inspiration was a game I used to play with myself when I was about nine or ten. I liked to imagine that a few friends and I survived a plane crash in a remote mountain wilderness and had to make everything we needed to survive from scratch, just like in *Robinson Crusoe*. I even played the game with my nephews when they were growing up. Now, Rufus is that kind of hero, someone who can figure out practical solutions to any problem. If he needs saddlebags for his bike, he makes them. He has the kind of resourcefulness and ingenuity I think Robinson Crusoe himself would admire!

Q. There are so many themes touched upon in *The Toothpaste Millionaire*—sexism, racism, age discrimination, entrepreneurship, friendship, finance, and math. Did you intentionally set out to include them all?

A. Ingenuity and friendship, yes. The other themes were not premeditated. But once I'd created the characters of Rufus and Kate, all the other themes came naturally into the story. Though, since I am not very fond of math, I had to work very hard at that part of the story. I had more pages of notes filled with numbers than pages with words!

Q. Why did you set the story in Cleveland, Ohio?
A. I visited a friend who had moved into an old middle-class neighborhood in Cleveland where there were a lot of black families. She didn't want her kids growing up in a white ghetto. She wanted them to know a cross section of people. I deliberately made Rufus a middle-class kid, not a poor inner-city kid, because in the 1960s many blacks had become middle class and had moved out of the inner city.

Q. There is a lot of humor and satire in your books. Do you have to work at being funny?
A. That's just the way it comes out. I never thought I was particularly funny. I can't even tell a joke right.

Q. What is the most important idea you hope readers will take away with them after reading *The Toothpaste Millionaire*?

A. I hope it inspires them to imagine themselves doing things like that. Just because they are kids, it doesn't mean they can't have good ideas.

Q. What were your favorite books as a child?

A. Louisa May Alcott's books—*Little Women*, *Little Men*, *Jo's Boys*, and so on. She got me thinking about becoming a writer. I also loved Albert Payson Terhune's dog stories.

Q. Were there any books you read as a child that you think particularly influenced you with regard to *The Toothpaste Millionaire*?

A. I remember finding some books by Horatio Alger on a visit to my grandmother's house when I was about twelve. They had belonged to one of my uncles when he was a boy. Written in the nineteenth century, they were all rags-to-riches stories about poor young men who worked hard, never gave up, and became big successes. So I guess that was an influence for *The Toothpaste Millionaire* too!

Q. What advice do you have for aspiring young authors?

A. Read, read, read. I never knew a writer who wasn't a reader first. When you read a lot you somehow assimilate what a good story is. And the things you read that move you will stay with you and help make you a better writer.

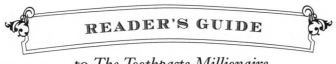

Book summary:

Rufus Mayflower and Kate MacKinstrey prove that you are never too young to have good ideas or succeed in business. Together they develop a simple recipe for toothpaste, manufacture, market, and sell their product, and make millions—all before the eighth grade!

Discussion questions:

An entrepreneur is a person who starts a business. Entrepreneurs have many qualities in common. What are they, and which of those qualities did you see in Rufus?

Starting a business is a difficult thing to do. What are some of the obstacles Rufus encountered in his efforts? What do you think made Rufus so successful?

Kate was extremely resourceful in finding empty tubes for toothpaste, the factory, and a foreman to run the factory. Do you think you would have been brave enough to do all that she did? How important is risk-taking in business? Is this any different from at school?

Rufus was clearly very good at math and engineering. Would you consider him a genius? Do you have to be one to be an inventor?

Kate said that math was not her strong point, yet she was still a good business partner. Why?

Rufus and Kate became friends after Rufus helped her pick up her books which had fallen into the street. Do you believe making friends is usually that easy? Do people have to have a lot in common to stay friends?

In the 1960s, when this story was set, Kate's character mentions that some people might think her friendship with Rufus was unusual because she was white and he was black. Do you think this could be an issue today?

Most of the book is told in the first person. However, chapter nineteen is written in the third person in the format of a movie script. The script dramatizes the price-fixing schemes of Rufus's toothpaste competitors. Why do you think the author chose to tell this part of the story in script form?

Throughout the novel, the author provides plenty of real-life math problems and walks readers through the steps of logical reasoning and calculation to solve them. How do you think this affects the storytelling? Did you try to figure out the answers to some of the math problems yourself?

At the end of the book, Rufus sells his business in order to have more time to think about what he would like to do next. Do you think this action is in character? Would you do the same?